MURDER, SWANS AND MISTLETOE

MAGNOLIA MOONE MYSTERIES
BOOK ONE

SABRINA DUVAL

Ballydoon
Books

MURDER,
SWANS,
AND
MISTLETOE

CONTENTS

Ballydoon Books

PO Box 1033

Oxley QLD 4075

Australia

https://louisaduval.com | hello@louisaduval.com

Fourth edition.

First published in 2023 in the 'My True Love Gave to Me' anthology as 'Seven Swans are Swimming' writing as Louisa Duval. The anthology was unpublished in May 2024 with all rights reverted back to authors.

The second edition is expanded and published under the pen name Sabrina Duval as an ebook.

The third edition is a duet with 'The Normie Next Door' and is a hardcover print.

ISBN: 978-1-7642311-0-7 - Paperback

READER NOTE:

This story uses US English and the authors have opted for US terms for common things. So you'll see neighbor, not neighbour. Color, not colour. If we got anything wrong, I apologize.

I cashed in my poetic license for phases of the moon. I was a full moon on 15 December, 2024 but I really needed a full moon for Solstice.

This is the first book of a series of murder mysteries with a modern spin on a fairytale. There is a promise of a happily ever after to come later and introduces you to the witchy side of life of Leavenworth, centered on a micro-brewery called Witches Brew and the witches who work there.

I hope you enjoy the first installment in the Magnolia Moone Mysteries.

CHAPTER
ONE

Winter solstice, for a witch, meant gathering around the fire with loved ones, a blessing under the moon for longer days to come, and eating excellent food and generally taunting your family members with hints of what you bought them for Christmas.

But Magnolia was pulling on her uniform for Pining for You, the local Christmas tree farm.

She had asked for this day off but when the manager called earlier, desperate for her to cover sick staff while they hosted the National Santa Championships, a wedding, and the usual crowds who wanted a white Christmas family experience, Magnolia agreed to come in.

She was also working at Witches Brew, as Magnolia had always done, growing up as a kid in Leavenworth, washing dishes, clearing tables, and now, managing the bar, including rosters, payroll, accounts, and assisting the chief brewer, her Aunt Aggie.

On top of that, she'd agreed to help with costumes and

props for the amateur theatre's Christmas play, "A Christmas Carol".

She was beginning to really feel the character of Bob Cratchit.

Wait, that was unfair. Magnolia only had herself to blame for agreeing to be everyone's dog's body and last-minute helper. More elf than witch these days.

A witch who didn't even have powers.

She plonked her bag, coat, scarf and knit cap on the kitchen bench and hugged Aunt Aggie.

"You're a good egg, helping out Pining for You like this," her aunt said. "But I'm worried you're stretched thin between here, and the Christmas tree farm and everything else you do—"

"It will all be over in a few days. Bring on Christmas. Ho. Ho. Ho."

"I hear your sisters are very keen to try a spell tonight to restore your powers amidst the National Santa Championships."

"They are." Magnolia pursed her lips before continuing. "The spell needs a special kind of fir tree and Pining for You has the right species, according to Prim so working there today fits in well with a little bit of spell casting. And not just the championships, there's also a high profile wedding on this year."

They were no stranger to big events and Christmas chaos but witches running around casting spells? Not so much.

In fact, speaking of witches, and warlocks, where was Uncle Vinnie? He was meant to be here helping.

"I know you're busy. More than busy but..." Aggie held up her hands, palms out, and channeled big 'hear me out' energy. "Would you mind picking up a Yule log for the hearth while you're at Pining for You?"

Magnolia's shoulders dropped a little. "Of course. What did you order from the farm?"

"Cherry wood. They have an old cherry tree at Pining for You and they pruned it back this autumn. They saved me a decent log from a bough and Geri has some mistletoe to dress it up before we burn it tonight. We can scatter the ashes on Twelfth Night."

To scare away evil spirits, Magnolia thought idly, and then shivered.

The Moone women burned their Yule log in the original hearth. In terms of history, the building was only just over one hundred years old and was built with a double fire place. One side was in the staff room of Witches Brew, and the other side had been bricked up. Their ancestor, Hilda, had settled in Leavenworth when it was a logging town and had created by accident the strangest room of all at Witches Brew; the *mutatio cubiculum* – literally Latin for the 'change room' because it transformed into whatever you needed every time you walked into it.

Sometimes it was a storeroom, other days a library with a comfy chair, and most recently, Prim used it as her office to coordinate CovenFest, the annual magic-user conference that was held in Leavenworth at Halloween.

After too many accidents over Witches Brew's one hundred year-plus history with a double fireplace that kept changing on one side over the years led to Great Aunt Agatha bricking it up in the 1950s.

So tonight would be celebrated in the staffroom with the Yule log burning bright, sipping hot cocoa, and telling stories of their ancestors from the family grimoires.

"Are you okay, sweet cheeks?" Aggie asked.

Magnolia had sighed loudly.

She tried to shrug it off but Aggie was too shrewd for that.

"What's on your mind, Magnolia?"

"Well ... what if I did get my powers back tonight?"

"That would be a good thing."

Magnolia sighed again. "I guess," she muttered.

Aggie frowned. "What's gotten into you? Restoring your powers back would be wonderful!"

Magnolia shrugged again. "But I was just a kitchen witch, Aggie. Essentially the Queen of Soup."

"You still are queen of soup. Our daily specials in winter sell out. Now, what's this all about?"

"At least Mum was a hearth witch, putting the magic into the mundane. The paranormal into the pedestrian. The arcane into the administrivia of things." Magnolia grumped. "Want a little spice in your tax return so the auditors look the other way when you made a creative claim? Boom, done."

Not there had been any boom magic-wise for twelve months.

Magnolia liked being a kitchen witch—*had* liked.

But tonight, a year on from an awful car accident where she woke up in a hospital with no familiar, no idea what had happened other than 'car go smash' and no connection to her craft.

"The hearth is literally the heart of a home. A hearth witch tends to the heart of her coven, her family, those she loves. Now tell that's mundane or pedestrian or whatever you said. And since the kitchen is the home of the hearth, some say the most powerful witch of all is a kitchen witch."

"I'm just feeling maudlin today. A year after the accident and all."

"That Rick got into your head, made you doubt your strength. Mark my words, Magnolia, you are more than soup, and stews and casseroles. The kitchen is the lifeblood of a house and you are the balance of this coven."

The balance. She'd been told that ever since she could remember.

"Balance of what? Kitchen scales for ingredients?"

"Ha. Ha." Aggie swatted her with a dish towel.

"One of the last things Mum said to me before she passed was at the heart of the hearth is fire, and without a fire, the hearth is dead."

"Very well put." Aggie paused. "A hearth witch brings different energies to one place. While Primrose is a green witch, through and through, your mother would call on nature to know what herbs to pick and when, and how to prepare them, she would lend an ear to those who needed it by the fire, and she also healed, whether it was filling someone up with soup and grilled cheese on an icy cold night, or specially baked *speculoos* cookies. A hearth witch is all these things, and a little more. It all starts in the kitchen and a hearth witch establishes a home for our cauldrons and our brooms."

"We Moones have a long history of being wanderers."

At this Aggie cackled and hooted. "Dearie, we are centuries and centuries of a family who fled, not wandered. Wandering makes it sound like we bumbled along at a shambles pace, like tourists. We escaped. We were refugees seeking sanctuary and safe harbor. It's been almost three hundred years since our ancestors skulked around in the *Schwarzwald*." Aggie preferred the German word instead of saying 'Black Forest'. "They were searching for solace and a place to practice our rituals in peace. But it's been here, in this weirdo fake Bavarian town in which we have found peace for the longest time. Can you believe it's been over one hundred years since your great-grandmother settled here in Leavenworth and established her hearth?"

"I think Leavenworth prefers quirky rather than weirdo." Aggie made a face. "On some days, the way the plumbing plays up, I can believe this place is over one hundred years. Even older."

Aggie rolled her eyes.

"Wait a sec, are you saying that one hundred years is the longest our family has stayed put in one place?"

"Correct. It's all in the Moone family grimoires." Aggie sighed and stirred her tea. "Magnolia, I've always said it, as did your mother and father, you are the balance in this family. The heart. And you still are even with your powers currently missing."

Missing was an interesting way to put that Magnolia's ability to wield the craft had evaporated, been obliterated. Missing sounded like she now only had one sock.

Missing sounded like she was a cat that had wandered off.

Wandered. That word again.

She chose to ignore her aunt's pep talk and pressed her for more family history. "Aggie, how did our ancestors know when it was time to move on?"

"To flee, you mean? Ha! When they came at us with pitch-forks and fiery torches. When someone in power took a dislike to us and made things difficult." Aggie squinted at Magnolia. "Why do you ask?"

It have never occurred to Magnolia to ask before, until now. She shook herself again, and then gave in to Aggie's question. "It just feels like ... the build up to a storm. Like there's some-thing on the horizon, just out of sight, but it's coming."

Aggie's face fell. "You should talk to Aspy, share your concerns."

Magnolia shook her head, laughing. No one just talked to Aunt Aspidistra, and certainly no one would ever call her Aspy to her face.

"Aggie, I have no powers. This feeling, these jitters, it's all just in my head. Paranoia. Exhaustion with the Christmas rush. Maybe it's even a real storm. Have we checked weather reports?"

"I don't believe you've lost your powers," Aggie murmured. "I believe you've lost how to connect with them."

Her aunt's low tone was unsettling. Magnolia tried to laugh it off. "Same, same, really."

"No, what I'm saying is if you feel this way, then what you are feeling is real. This isn't jumping at shadows in a horror movie. Tell Aspy, promise me."

"But telling Aspy, I mean Aspidistra, will make her worry—"

"Good, that's her job. And mine." Aggie pushed her tea cup aside, and clapped her hands as if the matter was done with, and then picked up two cheese graters, and held them up posing as if she was a bad ass superhero, or villain, whose purpose was shredding blocks of *Emmentaler* cheese. Which, in a way, that was Aggie to the core. A cheese grating badass.

"The *Emmentaler* calls to me to reduce it to shreds." Aggie chuckled. "You should go. Your sisters are waiting and Prim has been preparing for this ritual this evening for weeks."

Magnolia lingered by the door, studying her aunt. "You don't think this is going to help, do you?"

Aggie put the graters by a block of *Emmentaler* and took up a wire and cut the block of cheese down the middle.

"Restore your powers? No." To hear her aunt admit this didn't sting as much as would have done six months ago. "I have other theories about how you could connect to your powers. But I think you need to do this with your sisters to reconnect. Sisters first, craft second. And collecting the Yule log is a very, very close third."

Magnolia smiled. "I am looking forward to running around Pining for You tonight. And having one of their hot chocolates, or two. Not so much National Santa Championships or drunk guests at the wedding. And I won't forget the Yule log."

"Good." Aggie shook a grater towards her for emphasis. "We'll set it up tonight when you're all back."

As Magnolia exited, Aggie called after her. "Oh! And Tonya stopped by very early. You were still asleep from your shift at Pining for You last night. Wants to talk to you about next year's Christmas play with the Leavenworth theater group."

"That can only mean one thing." Wanting Magnolia to help with another project. She groaned. "Thanks, I'll keep an eye out for Tonya about that."

Magnolia considered her tri-colored hair in the rearview mirror. Dark brown and ginger waves with a white stripe at the front.

She'd always had non-descript brown hair, neither too dark or too light. Just mid-brown.

But not since the accident one year to the day.

And she wasn't used to it. Catching her reflection in the corner of her eye, she'd jump at the colors in her hair.

And her aunts and sisters were convinced it wasn't a magical dye job. It appeared that the stress of the car accident —the shock or the fright of it?—caused her hair to change.

This was her hair color now—all three of them.

Witches Brew loomed in the reflection of her rearview mirror. That bar had been their sanctuary for over one hundred years.

Why, then, couldn't she shake the feeling that something was closing in, something in the shadows, just out of view?

Magnolia Moone was being scrutinized from head to toe by the most glamorous guest staying at 'Pining for You'. A Christmas tree farm with a coffee shop, gift shop stocked with every decoration you could think of, wedding function center, petting zoo, temporary reindeer farm, holiday chalets, and, of course, rows and rows of Christmas trees didn't often attract guests of Denise Astor-Browne's wealth.

Mrs. Astor-Browne was barely five feet tall and was immaculately dressed in a designer merlot-colored jacket and skirt. A white fur stole was draped around her shoulders, unironically. She also wore a scowl, also unironically.

Magnolia was drawn to the light bouncing off the multiple rings on Denise's fingers. Diamonds which could only be described as boulders glinted in the light, threatening to take out an eye if anyone came too close.

"I've been waiting over fifteen minutes for the manager and he's nowhere to be seen," Denise sneered.

Magnolia used her practiced customer service smile. Her

manager was seeing to another issue involving a fire extinguisher, gaffer tape and two dozen pink cupcakes.

Magnolia, instead, had come to answer Denise's urgent call. "I'm more than happy to help."

Mrs. Astor-Browne huffed, turning her back on Magnolia and expecting her to follow into the room.

"I saw you looking, girl." Denise held up her ring-cover fingers and waved her hand. "All this is paste. Fake. But that —" She pointed her multi-ringed finger to the coffee table where a tiara sat on a velvet box. "That *is* real, and I need to know how to secure it in the safe before I attend the wedding reception."

A pug stood wheezing beside the coffee table. It winked and then plonked down on its butt. "Woof."

Uncanny, Magnolia thought. It sounded like the dog had faked its woof. Like it was saying 'woof' rather than actually woofing.

Denise clicked her fingers. "Are you listening, girl?"

"My name is Magnolia," she murmured and then turned her attention back to Densie. "Your pug is adorable."

"My niece gave him to me as an early Christmas present. Last thing I need is a pet. But here we are, aren't we Pugsley?"

The dog seemed to narrow its eyes—quite an achievement for a bug-eyed pug. "Woof, woof."

"Hmmph." The woman waved at Magnolia to come closer to the wardrobe where the safe was wide open. "Anyhoo, time to get this safe to work for me."

"Ma'am, are you sure you want to keep your jewelry in there? The manager has a larger, stronger safe in his office with an alarm system and CCTV."

Denise huffed. "I will not have this out of my room, young lady."

At thirty-six, it had been a long time since Magnolia had been called young.

She clicked the safe shut and Magnolia poised her index finger ready. "What code would you like, ma'am?"

Denise shrugged. "Oh, I don't know. Choose something, will you?"

Magnolia bit her lip, and then relented. It was against the rules to set safe codes for guests, but she chose the path of least resistance and set a four-digit code and the safe beeped.

"Okay, your code is 3125. And you need to press this button before you enter it, and then the hash symbol—"

Something rustled outside the chalet and the pug growled, its hackles up.

"Go and see to it, girl." Denis waved her towards the sliding door to the private patio of the deluxe chalet.

With the pug by her side, Magnolia threw back the curtains and a raccoon fell off the outdoor table.

"Just a raccoon." The animal grizzled and then scurried away. Magnolia glanced at the gathering clouds overhead. "And it looks like snow tonight. You should keep this door locked, ma'am."

The pug kept growling.

"I know how to keep a door closed," Denise tutted. "You may go now. Thank you."

Magnolia shared a look with the pug who rolled its eyes—or was struggling to focus, it was hard to tell—and then left without another word.

Her mobile beeped with several texts from her boss, and she idly read the last one.

> Boss: Champagne needed in 10 at wedding for bridal photos

And another text.

> Tonya: Heya! Missed you at the bar today. Anyhoo would love to talk to you about being involved in our Christmas play next year. Am thinking The Nutcracker! Like the ballet! Talk soon xx

Magnolia groaned and left Tonya on read. Anything to do with Christmas next year deserved to go unanswered while Christmas this year had yet to pass.

She opened two texts from Prim.

> Prim: Brayden is playing drums at the wedding at Pining for you tonight so I called in some favors with staff to run the bar with Aunt Aggie tonight. No sign of Vinnie

Huh. Brayden was a relatively new hire as a bartender and he also played drums for Geri's band on occasion, too. But it was the second text that made Magnolia sigh.

> Prim: We're here and ready. Where are you? We are losing valuable time. Moon's out, Yule is on, time to get our spell on.

Just another witchy winter Solstice at a Christmas tree farm.

"SHOULD BE AROUND HERE, SOMEWHERE." Magnolia pivoted at a cross section at the heart of Pining for You between advanced spruce and pine trees. A small wooden sign declared one way for spruce and another way for conifers. "I think. The owner doesn't have signs for the rare trees. He's had problems with theft."

Geri, short for Geranium, frowned. "People steal rare pine trees? Really?"

"Absolutely, just like how people sometimes steal rare flowers from you." Prim surveyed a row of spruce. "And don't get me started how digging up the bulbs in the middle of the night is a thing. So I'm not surprised about rare trees at all."

Geri was a florist. Not a green witch, she liked the artistry of flowers rather than growing them. Her strength in magic was divination and performed readings at her florist shop.

Her flower business all but halted in winter except for one kind of plant.

Mistletoe. Prim had agreed to grow and supply all kinds of mistletoe for the Christmas season from their family's apple orchard, Little Red Orchard.

"I bet the wedding couple loved your mistletoe table arrangements for tonight," Magnolia said.

"They absolutely did," Geri said matter-of-factly, tossing her flame-red hair over her shoulder, showing off her mistletoe corsage on her coat lapel. Magnolia and Prim wore matching corsages as well. "I went with North American, European and the Spanish variety *Viscum cruciatum* for its red berries and leaves. Paired with stemless white roses sourced from down south, which is a classic wedding bloom."

Geri took a deep breath as Prim murmured under her breath, "here she goes."

"Mistletoe is not just for Christmas, it's also a symbol for coming together as a couple and for healing, like they say in wedding vows 'in sickness and in health' and I guess in romance. Mistletoe could totally be a flower of choice for Valentine's Day. And, certain varieties were used in ancient times for medicine, not the poisonous ones, of course, and some were used in spells. Including the poisonous ones."

Prim hummed in appreciation as Magnolia cried out.

"Ow!" She sucked her fingertip and scowled at her corsage. "I think you've made weaponized wedding decorations."

"Don't eat the leaves or red berries. They're poisonous." Magnolia blanched, staring at her finger with its pinprick of blood, but Geri waved off her growing panic. "You'll be fine. It was a scratch, not a degustation meal of the plant."

"Why does healing, love and medicine have to be so prickly?" Magnolia grumbled, wrapping her finger up in a tissue and hoped she wasn't about to die.

Death by corsage. What an entirely underwhelming way to go.

Prim loomed in front of her, looking like Morticia Addams' twin sister. "Do you want to be selling Christmas trees for the rest of your life?"

Magnolia stood her ground. There was a charm to selling Christmas trees. Families getting their first ever real tree. Grandparents buying a special tree in anticipation of their first grandchild coming to stay at Christmas. Couples buying their first tree together.

Her heart stuttered. No, the couples were the worst. They reminded her of what her ex, Rick, had promised and never delivered.

"A green witch asking me if I have a problem selling trees as a lifelong career choice?"

"I, personally, have no issue with that. But you are not a green witch, dear sister."

"Aunt Aggie asked me a similar question before I came here. Did I want to serve beer and cider for the rest of my life at Witches Brew?"

Nothing was wrong with helping Aunt Aggie brew beer and cider, and run her micro-brewery and bar in Leavenworth, only thirty minutes by good roads from the Christmas tree farm. Nothing was wrong with selling Christmas trees, or decorations, or hot chocolates either.

Her sisters exchanged a look. "This is about your lack of

witch powers. And you know it," Geri said matter-of-factly.

Magnolia had been the witch that others once turned to for advice and mentorship. Now she fobbed off any witch who approached her about spells or joining covens. Her sisters and her aunt had kept her loss of powers secret for the last year. Discreet enquiries were made with some of the most powerful witches from all corners of the world at CovenFest, but nothing came of their suggestions. Her secret wouldn't stay secret for long. Soon, the global witch community would find out.

"Prim had a good idea for a spell to bring back your powers. It's been a year since the day you lost them. And we need a bough from a rare spruce, not pine," Geri called out over her shoulder, pulling Magnolia out of her thoughts. "Norwegian spruce should do it nicely and I think we'll find it ... that way."

Magnolia hesitated as her sisters charged down a row of perfectly shaped Christmas trees.

She glanced at her phone. Her manager had texted a second time about champagne for the wedding and could she pop into the coffee shop to check on stocks when she had a moment.

Her sisters had charged off down the row of trees.

Magnolia called out. "Why rare spruce? And you're going to pay for what you use, right?"

Prim and Geri stopped and ushered for her to catchy up.

"It's been a year since losing your powers." Prim ticked off her fingers. "We're witches, and it's Yule, and that's auspicious."

Ever since Magnolia was T-boned by a speeding vehicle a year ago that had knocked her hatch and the U-Haul trailer she'd been towing onto their sides, and had left her bleeding across the bitumen. Fleeing Rick and his abusive behavior.

Magnolia shuddered. That word again: fleeing.

Ever since that horrible car accident on December 21 last year, her powers had been on the blink.

Zip. Zero. Zilch.

She was a normie now, at thirty-six-years old. Mundane. Just an everyday person.

"And witches do not sell Christmas trees," Prim declared, ticking off her pinky finger and shaking Magnolia out of her thoughts.

"They do too," Magnolia protested. She was the top selling employee at Pining For You. "If Geri can sell flowers, I can sell pine trees, am I right, Geri?"

But her sister wasn't listening. Geri was sniffing the air as an icy breeze whipped up. "Oh, here we go." She picked up her pace through the snow in the opposite direction. "I can smell it. The spruce we're after. Can you smell it, too, Prim?"

Reluctantly Magnolia followed. How could Geri sniff out a rare tree?

But then again, Geri was surrounded by flowers all day, every day. Maybe she did have a superior nose for sniffing out trees.

"No other spells have worked so far," Magnolia reminded them.

Geri cleared her throat. "Magnolia, what is Yule?"

"An old Norse meaning the twelve-day pagan winter festival." Magnolia pouted. "And then later adopted and assimilated into Christianity. As you are both very aware. And you didn't answer my question. Why tonight when no other spell has worked."

Geri paused her tree sniffing. "Prim had an idea. And Aunt Aggie agrees with her."

"What idea?" Well, Aggie had kept that to herself. "What's worth a shot?"

Prim folded her arms. "Didn't you read our texts?"

Magnolia winced. "No? It's been insane with sales and the wedding tonight. They released doves at the end of their ceremony. I was dove-minding half the day, you know. Then, there's the National Santa Championships where we had five trays of cookies go missing. And we had a complaint about a nesting pair of swans by the pond as well as chasing a raccoon from a guest's chalet after they caught it going through their bin."

Her sisters were not overly impressed with my bird wrangling skills or event planning support to Christmas wedding brides and grooms or creative efforts of trash panda control.

"We've tried everything," Magnolia reasoned. "And the last time we tried a spell, I was discovered naked in the middle of a salt circle charging my crystals under the full moon by the deputy sheriff who arrested me for indecency."

"Yeah, but he didn't press charges," Prim smirked. "Didn't Brad ask you out?"

"Repeatedly. He won't stop texting."

Geri sniffed the air again. "Aunt Aggie insisted we do this on Yule under the moonlight. You lost your powers on Yule and year ago, and thus, we can restore the balance on Yule as part of an annual cycle, yadda yadda."

"I love the long night. The darkest night of the year." Prim's face lit up. "And as the legends say, the night of the Wild Hunt."

Geri waved her hand and continued to sniff the trees. "And in conclusion, we need a special tree for a Yule log."

"That's sorted. Cherry wood. And I've been working on an incantation based on the Wild Hunt."

The chances of the Fae Queen scooping them up for a romp in the middle of the night on Yule were incredibly small, but you never knew your luck in rural Washington.

"You can't just take a branch off a rare tree," Magnolia blurted as Geri tugged a little too hard at a spruce. "You have to buy the whole thing."

"I intend to." Geri nodded. "This one will be great. After we perform the ritual, Aggie said we can put it up in the bar. And on the twelfth night of Christmas, I'll burn it as a bonfire at the apple farm. It will be a symbol of how we restored you to full witchy health and the ashes will be scattered for good luck in the new year."

To tell the truth, Magnolia would rather skip this ritual and watch *Buffy the Vampire Slayer*, eat chocolate and heat up leftovers from the bar. Aunt Aggie had promised to save a serve of roast pork with vegetables and gravy, and homemade apple sauce from tonight's special at Witches Brew.

Magnolia sighed. If only she'd left minutes earlier that ill-fated Yule night twelve months ago. Five minutes earlier or later would have made the difference.

Magnolia would still be a witch with powers, and she'd be in a coven with her sisters, and not traipsing around a Christmas tree farm in the hope of finding a rare tree to perform a spell.

Geri produced a white cloth from one coat pocket, a moonstone – apt for the three sisters of the name Moone – and a curious clear potion that Geri said had taken two weeks to make and wouldn't say another word about it, and a knife.

Prim held up a pair of deer antlers she'd found in the woods during their molt. "To invoke the favor of Diana, goddess of the hunt," she explained with a grin.

"And now," Geri said with a flourish. "We need the moon."

They looked up at the cloudy sky and collectively sighed.

"Do you really need me to have my powers back?" Magnolia sighed.

Geri and Prim exchanged a look.

"Mags, we miss you and we miss our coven, and we know you do too." Prim sniffed.

Geri could control air, which meant she could sing like a siren and influence the weather with wind. Prim had the powers of earth and nature, growing apples, and mistletoe, of nurturing all kinds of plant life.

"And then there's you, Magnolia, you're ... the balance," Geri said softly. "You always have been the one who kept the balance of power in our coven. And, put simply, you're a witch whether you cast spells or not."

Magnolia snorted. What was a witch without powers? A normal everyday tax-paying citizen.

She swiped at her eyes. "We have all night to do this, right?" she asked, pulling out her phone again.

There were more texts pinged from her boss, each increasing in their anxiety. The last one was about a biting reindeer causing havoc with the Santa Championships.

"You guys stay here, and I'll attend to some workplace issues, and I'll be right back to chant my way to get full powers again on a waning full moon on Yule."

Magnolia dashed off to the protests of her sisters.

Workplace dramas she could deal with.

The chances of getting her powers back, however, were slim-to-none at best.

"It's going to be great," Brad enthused over Derek's car speakers. "It's a wedding, man. Lots of people meet others at weddings. Great place to find a date."

"Sure sounds like something." *Like desperation*, for example, Derek thought, as he parked his car in the back corner of the extensive car park at Pining for You.

"This wedding is a year to the day since your divorce came through and you haven't dated anyone since."

Derek stumbled as he climbed out of the car and held his phone up to his ear. "How did—"

"My cop spidey senses. That's why they made me Deputy Sheriff. Tell me I'm right."

Derek adjusted his coat over his tuxedo and then scanned the car park for directions to the function center. "I haven't been in any rush to jump into a relationship after Suzanne."

"She really did a number on you."

Brad was partly right. But Derek remembered all too clearly how often his ex had accused him that he was more married to his job as a detective than to her. And part of him agreed with her. The other part desperately wanted to change, hoped he actually had this last year.

"All I'm talking about Dez is going on a date. One measly date."

His cousin had met an apple farmer a year ago at Pining for You, just thirty minutes detour from Leavenworth, and two and a half hours' drive from Seattle. A year later, she was marrying the love of her life at the place they met in the function center.

Derek had worked with Brad just shy of two decades ago as fresh recruits in the Seattle PD. But Brad moved to Chelan County ten years ago wanting a rural lifestyle and had worked his way to become the deputy sheriff in Leavenworth. Brad was very good friends with the apple farmer, and now here they were, dressed in penguin suits and surrounded by the spirit of Christmas.

"Well, I'm dressed to impress." Brad's phone distorted for a second. "Might meet a new lady friend this evening. Thought I was a shoo-in with a local girl just this last week, but she blew me off. Where are you anyway? They're getting photos done so we have time for a drink."

The ceremony had been held earlier at Pining for You, but Derek couldn't get time off to be here for it. He'd pushed the speed limit as it was to arrive now for the reception.

"I'm parked." Derek looked around again for a sign and gave up, and chose a path flanked by life-sized nutcracker soldiers. "I'm just walking up now."

"Great, let me convince you to quit the big city and join Wanatchee PD in rural Washington over the best cider you've ever had."

They ended the call, avoiding the eyes of each nutcracker,

and instead inspected each of their brightly painted rifles and swords. He'd left his police-issued gun in the glovebox of his car, determined for one night to be Derek the wedding guest, not Derek the detective. He felt his tux's inside pocket where his badge was stowed. Some habits don't stop for a wedding.

He was about to follow one path and then abandoned that direction for another when he ran into another man.

"Sorry, didn't see you there." Derek seized the man's shoulders to avoid faceplanting the path, or a nutcracker soldier.

"Get your hands off me," the man hissed, as something his wallet fell open on the path.

Derek beat him to pick it up and handed it to him, not before Derek caught his name. Lenny Siddler.

For a split second, Derek thought it was Lenny from his favorite band, The Vice. Brad had told him the band were using Pining for You for auditions after Christmas.

But another look at this guy with the dark circles around his eyes, his hunched shoulders and short stature, Derek realized Mr. Siddler was nothing like the guitarist.

"No harm done. Again, sorry about that."

Lenny snatched the wallet and stalked off. "All the same with you penguin-suited snobs."

Derek paused, putting some distance between him and the delightful Lenny, who was overflowing with the Grinch spirit this early evening.

Snowflakes began to fall. Christmas trees and outbuildings then lit up with fairy lights. And Derek admitted it was rather romantic in a Christmas kind of way.

He held his breath and waited ... and ... no pangs of regret, no ... anything. No guilt. That was good. Maybe this was the perfect time and place to turn over a new leaf and meet someone new.

"Into the breech." He mock-saluted a nutcracker with

sequins on his lapels and then followed the festive path in the direction of noise and people, and opposite in direction to the surly Mr. Siddler.

Derek was definitely not at a wedding.

He was stuck somewhere much worse.

He was trapped in the interconnecting doorway for the coffee shop and gift shop of Pining for You. And he wasn't being melodramatic. Six carolers singing *Jingle Bells* were blocking his only exit, leaving him to politely listen and people watch. All around him were families shopping for ornaments, tinsel and gifts while couples huddled close to each other sipping hot chocolate and watching the snowflakes gently fall.

One couple was particularly couple-y. The woman had cream on the tip of her nose and the man with her couldn't stop laughing. He knew that look on the guy's face. He was head over heels. Smitten.

Ah, Christmas. The season of the couple. Derek hadn't been fully prepared for this onslaught of wholesome outpouring of love and togetherness.

He, a forty-year-old lonely divorcee at a Christmas wedding in a rental tux, should have seen this coming.

Derek tugged at his tie as he turned away from the hot chocolate couple. There must be another exit somewhere. This was fast turning into the Case of the Missing Wedding.

Or rather, the Case of the Very Lost Wedding Guest.

His elbow clipped something near the door as he moved.

"Freeze," a feminine voice demanded behind him. "Do *not* move a muscle."

For a spilt second, Derek regretted leaving his gun in his car.

Was someone really trying to rob him at a Christmas tree farm's gift shop, full of witnesses?

And not only was his tux a rental, but he had the sum total of eight dollars in his wallet.

Derek shifted to the side to eyeball the woman. "What is going—?"

"I said. Don't. Move. A. Muscle."

She was a dark brunette with a ginger red stripe and a silver-white stripe in her hair, and was dressed in a forest green puffer jacket to her knees with the Pining for You logo on the lapel.

She also had several eggs in each hand. A second later, Derek realized the eggs were intricately carved with festive motifs like snowflakes, the outline of a stag's head, Santa Claus.

For a robbery, this was his strangest yet.

"You just knocked a set of carved goose eggs off our display. And if you break any, it will cost you $1499."

The only body part Derek dared to move was his eyelids. He blinked rapidly.

Over a grand? For carved goose eggs?

He watched her careful movements, gently placing each egg back into a display box, and then retrieved one more that had snagged on his suit fabric and was precariously dangling by a literal thread at his elbow.

"You can breathe now," she said. "You're safe."

"Okay, thanks," he said and then cleared his throat. "Hi. Hey."

Derek swallowed a groan. He was so out of touch meeting women. Especially a very pretty woman who had just rescued him from a clumsy, four-figure mistake.

That jolted him out of his stupor. "Do they really cost over a grand?"

She nodded. "The local artist made a set based on the twelve days of Christmas. Big with Seattle tourists." She took in his outfit in a slow look up and down. "And probably people in tuxedos," she added.

It was then he noticed her name tag. And a trolley beside her packed with champagne on ice, glassware, and strawberries.

"Magnolia." Derek smiled. Why her floral name seemed fitting he couldn't figure out, but it did. "I'm Derek Deveney and I'm very lost and I'm hoping you can help me find the wedding reception on today."

"You're in luck. I'm on my way there now." She waved to her trolley, and Derek fell into step beside her.

I am lucky indeed, he thought, as they exited the coffee shop and gift shop and headed down another path, this time the lampposts decorated with garlands of mistletoe.

~

Magnolia

HEY WAS SUCH a stupid little word. Unsophisticated, unsurprising. Unremarkable.

And then this stranger—Derek—says 'hey' with his chocolate-rich, deep voice and her insides fluttered.

There hadn't been a fluttering in months. More than a year if she was being honest.

"So, hello." Magnolia gripped the trolley's handle tight. "Hey." *Ugh, that word again.* "Off to a wedding, then?"

Pull yourself together, Magnolia.

She couldn't have felt more different to him in his tuxedo

25

with her in her work puffer coat, her fleece leggings, and a knit hat with a red pom pom on top.

Derek suddenly fidgeted with his tie.

"Oh, wait. Stop. It's now askew."

They both paused on the path and Magnolia reached up out of reflex to adjust his tie.

He was watching her with those warm brown eyes of his. Observant and alert.

"Askew? Don't often hear that word."

Magnolia laughed. "If the last twelve months of my life had a theme, it would be askew."

"Same," Derek murmured. "But admittedly, it's better now. I think."

He smelled like spice. Cinnamon, and maybe a hint of orange. And starch. She quickly finished his tie and stood back, needing space between them. She really shouldn't be touching guests or sniffing them. Especially ones in tuxedos with dark, warm eyes.

"Thank you." He ran his fingers through his hair. He had silver at his temples, and it only enhanced how distinguished he looked. Another flutter. "Are you working tonight at the wedding?"

Was that a lilt of hope to his question?

"I work everywhere, everything, all at once. Ha. If you've got a Christmas crisis, I'm dealing with it."

Derek opened his mouth, but her phone rang, cutting him off.

"Hi, oh. Mrs. Astor-Browne. You got my cell number—what? Right ... someone stole your tiara?" Magnolia flicked her gaze at Derek and found him intently listening to her call. "I'll be right there."

She hung up as Derek spoke. "There's been a theft? Detective with Seattle PD. Sober, and happy to assist."

He pulled from his coat a kind of wallet that flipped open, just like the movies, and there was his ID and badge.

"Oh, really? Wouldn't you rather go to the reception?"

"To be honest, the Case of the Missing Tiara with the Mysterious Magnolia is far more enticing right now than a wedding reception."

CHAPTER
FOUR

He's attached, surely, Magnolia deduced. He was a good looking, tuxedo wearing man. More than likely had a wife and kids, and a dog. Like a golden retriever to match his hair color. A deep honey-brown of a golden retriever.

Magnolia shook herself. He was here alone, however. Impossible to tell if he was wearing a ring with his hands in his coat pockets.

Her text-to-voice robo-assistant spoke shrilly from her phone, jolting her out of her daydream:

Prim messaged where are you, Mags? Moon's out, time to get our spell out.

"Get your spell out?" Derek parroted, looking amused. "And Mags?"

"When I'm not the courier of champagne, making and selling cider and beer, cleaner, waitress, receptionist, porter, butler, Santa wrangler, concierge, and now, solving what's happened to a missing tiara, I am a pagan goddess and it's Yule."

Derek snorted but there was no derision or judgement in his eyes. He was simply amused. And he had a dimple on his left cheek when he smiled.

Focus, Magnolia Moone. There's a tiara at stake!

"Do you prefer being called Mags?" he asked, gently leaning into her and booping her name tag on her lapel. "Or Magnolia?"

She could smell the orange and cinnamon of his cologne again.

He leaned back, blushing slightly, as if shocked by his forwardness.

"Magnolia," she answered breathlessly.

"Then that's what I'll call you. Magnolia."

Were they flirting?

Any thoughts of flirting snowballed with the realization that she could be a prime suspect.

"Oh, I should tell you I set the safe for this client. I shouldn't have done that. Clients should set the code themselves but, well, you'll see for yourself, Denise Astor-Browne is formidable and rich and used to getting what she wants."

"Then I should ask you, as the attending officer, do you have an alibi?"

"I was getting my spell on." Derek frowned slightly. "I was with my sisters in the rare tree section of the farm, and then after that, I collected champagne from our kitchen, and then I was rescuing valuable carved goose eggs from a clumsy detective."

"Fair point, and duly noted."

Magnolia parked the champagne trolley outside of the deluxe chalet and knocked, causing the door to move.

"Unlocked," she mouthed to Derek who nodded and ushered her aside.

"Call out to her as if nothing is wrong," he whispered close to her ear.

The thrill of the chase: she was in the middle of solving a crime with an off-duty detective.

She nodded and stood straighter. "Mrs. Astor Browne? It's Magnolia. From before."

No sound.

Derek nodded once and then smoothly and silently opened the door without a sound, shielding Magnolia from any threat.

Chivalrous but annoying as she couldn't see anything.

But she did feel how cold it was in Denise's room. Beforehand, Mrs. Astor-Browne had the heat cranked up to tropical levels.

Derek scoped the chalet for an intruder or foul play with Magnolia at his back.

It wasn't until he stopped in the center of the room, and then looked over his shoulder at her with a raised eyebrow that she realized she'd been clutching his waist.

Magnolia immediately let go with a whispered apology and Derek searched the bathroom.

"Clear," he called out as the curtains by the patio door billowed up in an icy breeze.

"No wonder it's freezing in here. She didn't lock her door as I had recommended."

"Safe is open. Velvet box for jewelry on the floor. But her handbag is on the bed—dear Saint Nick! What's that?"

Derek jumped away from the bed as Pugsley shook himself on the duvet. "Woof," the pug said.

Derek blinked rapidly. "Could've sworn that—"

"He's faking how he woofs? I know, it's weird." Magnolia

scanned the cream carpet and hummed. "Pugsley, this is Derek. He's going to help us figure out what happened."

The pug looked dubiously at the detective.

"You two old friends?" Derek asked.

Magnolia gave the pug a quick scratch behind an ear. "Close acquaintances, aren't we Pugsley?"

"Woof."

Magnolia scanned the carpet. "There was a visitor." Small sodden tracks went from the patio door to the safe in the cupboard and then there was animal hair and more slush in the center of the room. "I wish you could talk Pugsley. I think you were a witness to a crime."

"Woof. Woof." Pugsley flung himself off the edge of the bed and nodded at the patio door. "Woof."

"Is he telling us something?" Derek asked in disbelief. "Like a bug-eyed Lassie?"

Pugsley huffed a sigh. "Woof."

Magnolia picked up a clump of the animal hair. "It's grey, and it's fur. Not black like Pugsley's coat."

"And there are tracks. Shoe prints and ... some kind of cat?" Derek said, and Magnolia joined him at the patio door. "A lynx maybe?"

The tracks looked like tiny hands in the fresh thin layer of snow. "Raccoon," Magnolia sighed. "There was a raccoon here when I set the safe combination with Denise and ... I think she charged off after a raccoon." Magnolia glanced back at the safe. "That maybe took her tiara?"

Derek sniffed as Pugsley wheezed harder. "And the thief just left all of the other jewelry?"

He waved towards the dresser in the corner that had all of Denise's shiny rings and pendants.

"All fake. Denise said so. The tiara was the only thing of value." Magnolia slid the patio door open, careful not to leave fingerprints just in case. "I'll follow the tracks and see if I can find her and the marauding raccoon."

"Wait, Magnolia!"

But Magnolia was already outside and jogging alongside the footprints in the snow, careful not to trample the tracks.

On instinct, she pulled out her phone and began videoing the trail.

"The footprints are headed to the pond here at Pining for You. I'm, um, recording this for evidence." She pursed her lips in the cold air. Maybe she should call her boss, or the local police? Or just forge ahead? "I'm going to call out for Denise now. Denise? Denise! Can you hear me?"

Her voice was snatched by the wind picking up off the pond. In the distance, guests were laughing and cheering while skating on the ice rink to music. But no reply from Denise.

Resigned, Magnolia kept filming as she picked up her jog again and skidded to a halt.

A raccoon was crouched behind a snow-covered shrub, its eyes wide with alarm. In the glow of a solitary lamppost, gemstones twinkled in a crescent between the animal's teeth.

She aimed the phone camera at the raccoon. "You're under citizen's arrest, you thieving trash panda—"

A hiss to her right made Magnolia's heart race.

And then she heard the *whump whump whump.*

Slowly she turned and saw it; a swan, just as she feared, beating its wings as a threat.

Behind it, another swan hissed, and five fluffy cygnets narrowed their eyes.

Seven swans all staring her way and looking very shifty.

At that moment, the raccoon shot off towards the function center's kitchen, the tiara glinting in the gloom.

Swans attacked when threatened.

Swans were remorseless.

And she was severely outnumbered.

Magnolia clutched her phone and took off after the raccoon, thankful the swan had decided it didn't want to give pursuit.

~

Thirty minutes later, Magnolia was cold, wet and, if she was honest, a little bored.

The chase after the raccoon and escape from the swan had been thrilling. It was the first time in a year she had felt alive.

She'd followed the raccoon to a dead-end alleyway behind the function center's kitchens. Derek had found her guarding the entrance and now the chase had turned into a stalemate with the raccoon refusing to come out. Magnolia and Derek were staked out behind the dumpster to catch the thieving furball.

Derek was also miffed she'd run off without him.

So Magnolia was ignoring him, miffed that the raccoon was playing hard to get.

And they were now waiting for animal control to show up, with Derek refusing to leave her alone.

Magnolia looked up and snorted. Geri had even decorated the alleyway from the gutter with mistletoe garland.

Derek's phone started to ring with Taylor Swift's lyrics *'haters gonna hate'* and he quickly took the call. Huh, the detective was a Swifty. A surprise.

"Sorry, Brad. I'm—what? When?" Derek frowned as he listened. "Right. I've been at Mrs. Astor-Browne's room, and we believe this has been motivated by theft of a valuable tiara." There was a pause and Derek looked at Magnolia. "I've been assisting one of the senior members of staff about the robbery. She's ... a pagan goddess, among other roles." His lips quirked before his frown descended again. "That's her, yes."

Oh no, let it not be Brad the deputy sheriff. Magnolia crossed her fingers behind her back.

"We'll be in soon. With the tiara. And we'll give statements."

He clicked off the call and looked into the dumpster alley. "I'm sorry I have to tell you this, but Mrs. Astor-Browne was found dead. By the pond's edge. They suspect murder."

"You can't possibly suspect me!" Magnolia retorted.

"I don't!" He pinched the bridge of his nose. "I watched you pursue the raccoon from the chalet. I know very well you didn't commit murder."

"You're cross at me though."

"I'm not."

"Are too."

"I am not." Derek exhaled loudly and several beats passed when he then asked, "Are you seeing Brad, the deputy sheriff?"

She snorted. "I swear on Santa's beard, no."

"He said he saw you ..."

"Naked. Under the full moon? He did. Doesn't mean I will ever date the deputy sheriff in this lifetime."

Derek nodded slowly. "Brad is ..."

"Over eager? Cocky? Some say arrogant?"

"You left out opiniated." He huffed a laugh and they exchange small smiles. "For all of your insightful observations of Brad's character, of which I agree wholeheartedly, he's been a good friend to me."

Derek cleared his throat, giving her side eye. "So, you are single."

"I may be." She stole a glance his way. "Why are you asking, detective?"

"No reason," he said quickly, looking back at the alleyway.

"Are you single?" she blurted without thinking.

"Yes. A year to the day since my divorce."

"I'm sorry."

"Don't be. Let me assure you that you don't have to be sorry for me at all. It's a good thing. Being stuck with you behind this dumpster right now is better than my marriage was two years ago when we separated." Derek looked her way. "I'm sorry. I'm not cross and being here has been surprisingly fun."

"Even with a murder? When you could have been at a wedding?"

"Even with a murder. And a theft. And definitely the wedding."

A comfortable silence descended as they scanned the alleyway for raccoon activity.

"Same for me," Magnolia added. "I left my ex a year ago today. In fact, today is Yule, and it's a problematic anniversary for me. I'd rather be hiding behind trash cans with you than wallowing over relationships past."

Their eyes locked.

"You've only just met me," he said, his eyes sparkling in the glow of the outside light. He swallowed hard and glanced away, blushing again.

His nervousness made him even more charming, if the tuxedo wasn't enough. Derek would be a good detective, working with victims of crime and witnesses putting them at ease.

He was calm and yet vigilant and ready to spring into action, even in his tuxedo.

He eased into a standing position and then offered his hand to her, which she took and stood as well.

And she didn't let go.

"In truth, I haven't seen anyone since the divorce," he murmured.

"Me, too. Since leaving my ex, I mean."

Magnolia's thoughts were like snow flurries; quick and spontaneous. How she wished for her powers back, for things to be back the way they were, for the man in the tuxedo to like her. Then, the clouds parted, and the moon came out, bathing everything in its silver light.

When had she drifted closer to Derek?

His full lips were so close now.

What was happening? Why didn't this feel wrong?

All she knew was she was about to kiss an off-duty detective while staking out a potentially murderous raccoon.

CHAPTER
FIVE

S everal things happened at once by the light of the full
moon.

First, they kissed.

The kiss was good. Very good.

So toe-curling, spine-zinging good that Magnolia almost forgot they were on a stakeout for a thief, and potentially a murderer as well.

Second, mistletoe thorns hurt, as she was well aware, thanks to Geri's corsage. And especially when contact with said thorns was part of a snow drift falling off the roof, sending a thorny ball of three kinds of mistletoe straight for your forehead when your mouth was engaged in the act of a very good kiss.

And third, transformation.

Two transformations.

The raccoon had burst from behind a trash can, dropping the tiara in the middle of the alleyway's entrance and squealing in surprise as the snow slid off the roof and onto Derek and Magnolia's heads.

Which brought their very good kiss to an abrupt halt.

And the raccoon turned into a man with a bone-cracking, skin stretching display. Which was very unexpected—even more unexpected when that man was Lenny Siddler, janitor at the local high school, and part-time football mascot, known petty thief, and Magnolia's high school prom date from almost twenty years ago.

Not her proudest moment.

At the same moment Lenny had appeared, Derek fell backwards with a yelp into a snow drift, and Magnolia had felt an unexpected but familiar tingle in her nose, like she was about to sneeze.

That sensation was how it felt to use magic.

It was the forewarning of her lost self – the ability to turn into the shape of her familiar.

She hadn't felt this tingle for a year.

As the mistletoe fell to the ground, grazing her forehead, and wet snow dribbled down her neck, Magnolia was mid-thought *'but I can't use magic anymore'* when she turned into a cat.

She caught her reflection in a glass pane of the kitchen door and hissed, hackles up. She was a calico to be precise; all ginger and black with the old splash of white on her fur, with her clothes and boots strewn around her.

Lenny the former raccoon bleated in surprise, and then quickly grabbed a trash can lid to cover himself up, and then rolled his eyes.

"Magnolia Moone," he grumbled, swiping her coat, turtle-neck and mini-skirt from the snow. "Bet your sisters are somewhere here, too. Feels ... witchy tonight."

Magnolia hissed. Lenny Siddler was stealing her clothes, she thought in horror. *Wait, what did he mean by 'feels witchy'?*

Oh god, Derek!

Oh god, was Lenny a ... *were-raccoon?!*

And what the broomsticks – he was acting like he knew she was a witch all along.

And holy Solstice – she had turned into a *cat!*

Derek moaned from his patch of snow as Moggy-nolia and Lenny both spied the tiara between them at the same time.

Luckily for her, Lenny was struggling to pull on her mini skirt. She pounced on the tiara and plucked it from the snow in her mouth – *her ... fangs? Oh my goddess, she was a CAT!* – and then took off in graceful leaps. Away from staff, wedding guests and detectives in tuxedos with full lips who really knew how to kiss and who did not need to see her or Lenny in their new forms.

How would she even begin to explain what had happened to Derek? *'Oh sorry, looks like your kiss turned me into a cat'.*

Wait, was that what really happened?

Maybe she was a were-cat?!

Too many questions, too many tiaras and too many murder suspects on her literal tail.

Lenny began his pursuit in mincing steps. *Ha, you can't leg it in a tight mini, Lenny,* she thought, rounding the corner of another building by the pond.

But Lenny was gaining speed and even a magical cat had its limits. She was wet and cold, and with the adrenaline wearing off, the tiara was heavy to cart about in her jaw.

Magnolia quickly trotted into the building beside the pond. The boat shed! Seven swan-shaped peddle boats bobbed silently on the freezing water, waiting for spring when families would take them out on the pond and have picnics on the lawn.

A familiar voice roared in her head. *"Who the hell are you? And why you in my body how dare you!"*

She almost dropped the tiara into the pond. *"Oh my God this is that you Gordon? Why are you in my head?"*

"Magnolia?" The longing and how her old familiar's voice cracked with emotion almost made her drop to the wooden floorboards.

Named Gordon after the famous celebrity chef, his favorite pastime had been looking up soup recipes on YouTube, watching The Great British Bake Off and watching Mr Ramsay call people 'an idiot sandwich'.

And now her familiar was back, and in her head, having a reunion conversation.

"You're alive! I'm out of the darkness." Gordon let out an almighty cat howl from deep inside her chest. *"I have been in the darkness for so long."*

The howl hadn't been of her doing. Was she in her cat-body, or was she in his familiar form?

Magnolia's moggy heart pounded against her ribs. *"What do you mean, darkness?"*

"The void, infinite black. Exile. But, you're here in my head and my body. I'm finally out of the darkness but you are smooshed in here with me."

"Gordon, I'm pretty sure I've just turned into a cat and you're back, but you now exist in my mind."

"I beg to differ. You are definitely smooshed into my demonic form and in my head."

Magnolia did not know how to process this with a tiara in her teeth, and a murderer on the loose, let alone whether she was, as her demon familiar had put it, smooshed into the same body as him.

"I thought I'd lost you the night at the car accident." She gulped a breath, as a wave of emotion threatened to overwhelm her. *"I'd lost all my connection with magic, including you, and I just assumed that you had gone forever."*

"I was flung into the darkness that night and I've been trapped there ever since, unable to break free until now. What happened now? What changed? Where are we?"

"I don't know why I'm in your body. Two minutes ago, I thought I was a were-cat-like-creature, doubting everything I knew about myself. Now I'm finding out that maybe we are in the same cat form. I don't know why, I don't know how you're here, I'm so very glad you are."

"Why is there something between your teeth what the hell have you got there?"

Gordon spit the tiara out and then yawned, stretching their cat jaw.

"It's a tiara, it's valuable and we don't want Lenny Siddler to get it. Oh, and there's been a murder, too."

Gordon picked up the tiara again in their teeth. *"Lenny Siddler? Your prom date? He's still hanging around?"*

"I just told you there's been a murder but you want to talk about Lenny? Unfortunately yes. It is that Lenny and you should also know he is a were-creature. He transformed into this monstrous-looking were-raccoon. Happened under moonlight. I'm absolutely sure that he is a were-creature."

"What in the spiral dance has been going on since my banishment?"

Banishment?

"He might be a were-coon but he's also a certified idiot. Any other threats I need to know about?"

"There's a cranky swan lurking around this pond earlier. Keep an eye out."

"Roger that. Oh yes!" Gordan did a zoomie, the tiara violently swinging against his chest—our chest? This was all so confusing. *"It is so very good to be back, my mistress. I am here to serve. Let's raise hell and banish the were-raccoon!"*

"Raise hell? You were the Nigella Lawson of cat-demon familiars who loved to make soup! And you want to raise hell?"

"I want to make up for lost time. Can't you feel it? The night air bristled with magic."

Sure enough, Magnolia could see it. The colors pulsated around the trees. Trails of what a normie would call pixie dust kicked up every time they moved.

It was intoxicating and suffocating at the same time, like she was squashed into a tiny costume for Halloween and claustrophobia was closing in, causing her panic to rise.

"You should also know that you're now a calico cat not a black cat," she blurted.

"What in the gates of hell does that mean when it's at home?"

"You know, black white and ginger mottled coloring. Curiously enough my usual black-brown hair now has a white stripe and a ginger stripe since the accident. Cats that have the three colors are known as calico cats and they're usually female. It's a sex-linked color variation."

"Well, everyone's going to have to get used to me being a male calico cat-cum-demon familiar, comprendé?"

But how could she have her familiar back when she *was* transformed into her familiar? *"Gordon, I lost my powers the night of the accident. I haven't been able to connect with magic since then."*

"That's just nonsense, there is power thrumming away. I can feel it, can't you?"

Magnolia had time to blink twice and she felt it; like static electricity, all the hairs on their cat body bristled.

Gordon shuddered. *"It feels ... different to before. I can feel death has walked here. And magic all around."*

There was a shout in the distance. Was that Derek?

Footsteps rapidly approached and it felt like all of Magnolia's senses were warped, bending to pinpoint the source of the noise. Was this what it was like to be a cat? Honing the senses like a predator felt so sharp. Her humanness made her feel like a bumbling fool.

"*Lenny* ..." she gritted out.

"*Right.*" Gordon growled out loud. "*Let's focus on this were-coon and potential murderer.*"

Sure enough, Lenny shambled around the corner, struggling in her mini-skirt, and she hissed.

"Give it here," he demanded.

She growled, baring claws, but did not let go of the tiara.

Lenny pulled back his hand. "So, Magnolia Moone is a witch. Long time, no see, Maggie. Rumor had it you lost your powers, but I see that's not true at all. Nicely played on the rumor, but not smart enough for me."

Magnolia let out another growl. Lenny had no idea in high school that she was a witch. She was absolutely sure of it. How on earth did he know now and also hear of a rumor about her lack of powers?

But she genuinely had no idea that Lenny was a raccoon – no, a were-creature. His transformation was very different to hers. Lenny's body jerked and trembled with bone-jarring movements as his shape shifted into a man.

But her transformation as a cat was more of an illusion.

Ugh, had Lenny been a were-raccoon the whole time in high school?

Oh no, had she taken a raccoon to the prom as her date?

She growled again. So, if Lenny was a were-creature, that required the oldest kind of magic – blood magic – and that needed the light of the ... moon.

Preferably a full moon. Like tonight. And the clouds would make that difficult for him.

Magnolia had a lot of questions, none of which she could ask as a cat. Including had he murdered Denise Astor-Browne for a tiara.

"Look, that cop-lover boyfriend of yours will be here any moment. Want him to know your little secret, Miss Kitty?"

Magnolia bared her teeth and hissed again, no small feat with metal jewelry in her mouth. Had Derek witnessed Lenny's shift from raccoon into a man?

"Okay, okay." Lenny licked his thin, blue lips, his eyes darting around nervously but always landing on the tiara in her mouth. "Tell you what, I'll swap you your clothes back for the crown? How does that sound, huh? Unless you want to chase me naked, Maggie?"

It's a tiara, you idiot, she thought.

Magnolia bobbed her head, mewling at the back of her throat.

"Was that a yes? I don't speak cat. Clothes for the crown?"

She bobbed her head again.

"Alright, first the coat." Lenny began shedding her clothes as moonlight streamed through a window in the boat shed, right where she was.

Lenny threw the coat in front of her, the corsage landing at her feet. Mistletoe and moonlight …

She pawed the corsage and winced when a thorn pierced her paw, cutting her toe bean.

"Ow! What the— what's happening?" Gordon demanded.

The tingle started again, like before with Derek, and it grew stronger, making her whiskers twitch. She threw the tiara into one of the swan peddle boats and braced herself.

"Not the void, not again. Please, Magnolia, I beg—" Gordon whined in panic.

"We can't beat him as a cat." Gordon began to protest but she continued, the tingling growing stronger. His desperation

44

and pleading was visceral—she could feel his anguish throughout her whole cat body. *"I will bring you back again. I promise."*

The tingling led to a sneeze, and then *poof!*

Bare broomsticks. She was naked and no cat demon was in her head.

"Holy tamales," Lenny blurted in shock, as he struggled to pull off her turtleneck.

"Turn around, Lenny!" In the distance, Derek called her name. "Hand over my skirt and turtleneck, now!"

Lenny held out her clothes with his back turned.

"Gotta say Magnolia, everyone says Geri is the hot one of the Moone sisters but—"

"One more word Lenny—" She swiped for her turtleneck and pulled it on. "And I'll turn you into a … a—"

She stopped. Time for questions, not idle threats. "So, you're a werewolf. But a raccoon?"

"Prefer were-coon, thank you very much."

"But that's impossible. There are no werewolves or were-anythings around here."

Lenny's body was faintly blue all over, but he didn't seem to care. "You witches think you know so much. That you're so much better than us."

Magnolia frowned. She didn't think that at all, considering that she didn't know there were such a thing as were-coons until now, and was certain her sisters didn't either. And better than were-creatures? They hosted a clan of were-bears and werewolves during CovenFest for the first time this year.

"There's many things the Moone sisters don't know about in Leavenworth."

The moonlight was still streaming through the boatshed's windows. Lenny stepped into the light and began his metamorphosis into a raccoon again.

This time his form was monstrous in the moonlight: half man, half-raccoon, all ... beast.

For a raccoon, he was huge this time, like he had channeled the size of him as a man into the shape of a raccoon. Lenny bared his teeth. They were sharp, nasty looking. Along with his clawed coon hands.

"So, Maggie. We had a deal. Where's the tiara?" he growled.

Crusty cauldrons.

Lenny leapt at her. Magnolia knew a thing or two about self-defense, thanks to classes she had taken after leaving her ex.

And Lenny, though hideous in this were-form, still had his slight build. She flipped him midair and brought him down onto the wooden floor of the boatshed, holding one of his arms behind his back.

"What's with the tiara?" Magnolia tightened her grip and Lenny squealed. "Why did you kill for it?"

"Kill?" he squeaked in his ridiculous raccoon voice. She'd expected a scarier voice for a were-creature. "I didn't kill anybody." She tightened her hold on his arm. "I swear to you, Maggie! Yes, I took it from her room, and she chased me. I dropped the tiara when the swan attacked me, but she went to pick it up, and the swan then went after her. I used that as my chance to swipe the tiara. When I did, the old broad was bobbing face down in the water."

Magnolia frowned. If Lenny was telling the truth, there was still a murderer on the loose somewhere on the Christmas tree farm. A feathered murderer.

"Why did you want the tiara?" She increased her grip. "The tiara, Lenny. Why?"

He squealed and squirmed a little. The rough boards couldn't have been comfortable against his nether regions.

"I overheard a guy at a bar saying there was this tiara-crown-thing and that it would be here at the wedding, and it was valuable, so I took a chance to get it and sell it on later."

All for money, typical of Lenny. He'd always looked for a way to make a quick buck like get rich schemes or selling on free stuff.

"Come on, I'm telling the truth. Let go!"

He wriggled in her grip and Magnolia was distracted enough that he slipped out of her grasp.

"Where is it? We had a deal, Magnolia." His raccoon hands curled up into fists. "We had a deal."

She swallowed hard. "I threw it behind you. Back there."

Magnolia pointed behind him to the back of the boat-shed. Lenny snarled, knocking aside oars and ropes, swinging to his left, then right. He was clumsy in his monster coon form.

Then, Derek called out again, much closer this time.

Magnolia sprung into action, away from the feral Lenny-Coon, and bolted for the swan boats. They were two by two, except for a broken boat on its side in the shed. The only thing restricting the peddle boats from drifting off into the lake was a simple rope strung across the entrance to the pond. Magnolia unhooked the rope, threw it aside, and then pushed each boat ahead until the tiara swan came alongside her, and she jumped in, leaving two boats behind, and peddled like her life depended on it.

Which, in a way, it did.

Derek ran into the shed at that moment, something hanging from his hand, and shouted in surprise as were-Lenny took a flying leap into the second-last swan boat, chittering wildly in frustration as his coon legs and hands were not suit-able for using the peddles.

Derek spotted her then. "Magnolia!" He shouted, jumping

in the last swan peddle boat before it floated away and joined their strange flotilla racing across the lake.

"Derek, I've got the tiara!" she called back.

Out of the corner of her eye, a swan was flapping its wings on the edge of the pond. Even at this distance, it was clear another was standing guard near the nesting box.

I nicked the tiara while it attacked the old broad...

Crusty cauldrons, an angry pair of parent swans. Of course. They thought the nest had been violated and were protecting their babies from an attack.

The tiara's owner had chased the raccoon right into danger.

She had a feeling Lenny had told her the truth.

There was a splash behind Magnolia. "Get off me, you rabies-infected pest!" Derek waved at were-Lenny now clinging to the side of his boat.

But another cloud passed in front of the moon.

"Arghhh crud!" Lenny muttered, his voice carrying over the water.

He leapt back into his boat with a bone-jarring sound but Magnolia wasn't concerned about a naked Lenny. One of the swans was flying across the pond, straight for her.

"Derek, get down!" she yelled, twisting her body to fit into the footwell of the swan boat just as the swan flew over, beating his wings several times before gaining height and flying away.

The old broad was bobbing in the water...

Lenny was chanting now while turning his boat around. "I'm too young to die, I'm too young to die." He then dived into the freezing cold pond and swam to the boatshed.

The monster was terrified of the water bird.

Derek's long legs and frantic peddling had caught him up with Magnolia's boat. "Are you—?"

"I'm fine." She looked about her. "Where's the swan?"

Magnolia heard it before she saw it – the *whump* of its wings pumping the air in flight.

"Duck!" Magnolia crouched again, pulling Derek down with her.

This time one wing hit them both and she had to say it hurt.

"Don't you mean 'swan'?" Derek quipped, looking nonplussed but leapt into her boat with an impressive display of grace and agility and immediately cupped her face looking for injuries. "Are you alright?"

"I'm fine, really. I think the swan drowned Mrs. Astor-Browne. Lenny took the tiara while she was fending off the swan. He said the owner was bobbing in the water when he took the tiara from near the swan's nest."

"Murder swan?" Derek asked, incredulous. "And why is Lenny naked?"

She winced. "Long story. But yes, murder swan. Where is it? We need to get off this pond immediately."

A high-pitched scream made them both turn. Lenny had his hands in the air facing off her sisters in the boat shed.

"We've got him, Mags!" Geri called from the boat shed.

Prim grinned, holding Lenny down on the pier coming out of the boatshed with her boot. Green vines were crawling over Lenny. "I can apply pain, just say the word!

Relief was short-lived for Magnolia. "Where's the—" she began to shout back but stopped. "Oh no."

It was too late. The swan was right upon them. Magnolia ducked down but Derek wasn't as fast. He was caught off balance and tumbled out of the boat and into the water.

"Derek!"

The pond was near freezing for Yule, the longest, darkest day of the year.

Magnolia scrambled to the side of her boat as he came to the surface, spluttering and gasping for air with the shock of the icy water.

"It's coming back!" Prim called from the boat shed, pointing across the pond.

Magnolia took cover in the footwell again as Derek clung to the side. The swan skidded to their boat, beating its wings. Derek slipped under the water again.

Magnolia felt her panic rising. He couldn't come up to breathe again if the swan was beating its wings, holding him under.

That's how the swan had done it; chased Mrs. Astor-Browne into the water and then held her under until she drowned.

Magnolia could hear her sisters calling out, but everything faded into white noise.

She had to help Derek.

You are the balance ...

Prim was the earth and nature. Geri was air, and Magnolia was ...

"More than damn soup," she muttered.

She needed her sisters. As if on cue, Geri flung out a hand and blasted the swan away with a sudden gust of air but it landed safely.

But Derek was still underwater.

Exposure in freezing water could kill you so quickly, especially if he had water in his lungs.

No!

Magnolia seized the tiara. Diamonds are formed under intense temperatures and pressure in the depths of the earth, right? *And I'm still wearing Geri's corsage ...* She then locked eyes with Geri, and then Prim, as her hand curled around the mistletoe corsage, pricking her palm, and then plunged her other hand with the tiara into the water, thinking only of the power of three.

"Cauldrons don't boil without a fire," she murmured.

That tingling zinged through her again. Gordon didn't speak to her in her mind so she focused on the tingling, thinking only of burning a Yule log in the Witches Brew hearth with her sisters, and aunt.

Magnolia didn't know she'd closed her eyes until she opened them to find the pond rippling and bubbling. Steam rose from the surface as Derek burst up, grabbing her swan boat, gulping air.

She wrenched the corsage from her jacket in surprise and dropped it into the pond, and then flung the tiara aide into the footwell to grab hold of Derek's tuxedo jacket, almost sobbing in relief.

"Where's the murder swan?" he moaned.

The swan had flown back to its family and the nesting box, eyeing off their boat.

"It's gone, it's okay, I've got you." Magnolia grunted, pulling him into the boat.

Derek flopped into the peddle boat, coughing and spluttering. "The water is ... warm. Almost hot."

Dusty grimoires. He was right. Without thinking, she'd almost boiled a pond. She hoped she hadn't killed any fish with her insta-heat of the water.

Need to distract the detective ... His forehead. She gently pushed his wet hair out of his eyes and inspected a cut.

"Are you okay? Any more scrapes?"

Derek shook his head slightly but didn't ask her to stop. "I was looking everywhere for you. I heard shouts, then noise and then Lenny looking ... are you okay?"

The man had almost drowned, thanks to a murderous

swan and yet he was worried about her. His kind eyes travelled over her face, searching for evidence of injuries.

"I'm fine." Magnolia grinned, unable to stop stroking his face.

She was more than fine, she was buzzing. She'd connected with magic again!

"Did we, um, just solve a murder and stop a theft?"

"Magnolia Moone, I believe you did."

CHAPTER
SIX

The coffee shop was busy and warm, as Magnolia waited for her manager at the back to get a key for an empty chalet so she could have a hot shower before heading back to Leavenworth with her sisters. Magnolia's manager was beyond thankful for how she'd gone above and beyond for Pining for You, and had found a spare puffer jacket and clothes

Magnolia had given her statement to the police as best she could, knowing Lenny wouldn't tell them she was a witch. Who would believe him? And she knew he knew she couldn't very well tell normal people *'Lenny Siddler is a were-raccoon.'* She'd let the moonlight expose him should the heavy cloud cover clear.

But, there would absolutely need to be a future conversation with Lenny. An interrogation of sorts.

As well as with her sisters. Tonight, as soon as possible. About her powers, the moonlight and the mistletoe.

Geri had said that some kinds of mistletoe were used for

medicine and healing. Magnolia couldn't help but wonder if that was a catalyst for connecting with her powers.

And Gordon. She had to get her long lost familiar back, and in his own cat body.

And then there was the issue with Lenny. Did Prim and Geri know about were-creatures running around Leavenworth? And how did he know she was a witch?

So many questions. An urgent cauldron congress was needed over leftover roast pork back at the brewery with Aunt Aggie.

At first, Magnolia thought the man in the tuxedo approaching her was Derek. But it was an older man she'd never met, with more silver than brown hair, and a moustache.

"Excuse me, you must be Magnolia Moone?" She nodded. "Please allow me to introduce myself. I'm Chuck Dawson. I was a guest at the wedding tonight, and I just spoke to Derek Deveney before he had to leave. He told me about tonight's arrest." He paused and said in a low voice. "And unfortunate loss of life of a guest."

She nodded again. Magnolia's heart sank. Derek had gone? Without saying goodbye?

"Did you know Denise—?"

"No. Not at all. But it was very sad what happened."

"She was not a well-liked woman. To say she was difficult is saying it nicely." Chuck gave her a rueful smile, and then held out his card. "I own a private investigation firm in Wanatchee and provide services to the local counties. I'm looking to hire more PIs for the work we do. It's not always as interesting as jewelry heists or murder cases, but Derek said he thought you had personal qualities that made a good PI."

Magnolia traced the embossed words 'Dawson and McIntyre, Private Investigators' with her finger. "He did?"

Chuck nodded. "Well done, tonight. Please feel welcome to get in touch if you are interested."

"Thank you," she murmured, pocketing the business card.

As Chuck said goodbye, her boss hurried over, carrying two jumbo-sized hot chocolates.

"Everything okay with the guest?" he asked nervously, handing her one of the cinnamon spiced warm mugs.

"Yeah, he's fine."

"Wildlife Control will be here in the morning to remove the swan family. Police have fenced off the nesting box around the pond and will patrol tonight." Her boss settled into his seat and then slid a key across to her for a chalet. "Every year there's mayhem of some kind but a murder swan tops it all." Her boss scanned her face. "You're not coming back to work for me, are you?"

Magnolia slowly shook her head. "Sorry. It was the murder swan that did it. Thank you for having me for the last twelve months while I've been back in town."

Her boss sighed. "To be honest, Magnolia. You're one of the best employees I have. Nothing fazes you. Not even tonight."

Magnolia smiled. "Can't say it wasn't interesting though."

"I'll pay you out to Christmas Eve. Least I can do."

She held up her mug for a toast. "Thank you and may your Christmas be murder-free."

"Done." And they clinked their mugs.

DEREK KNOCKED on the chalet's door. Pining for You's manager had been obliging to let him know where Magnolia was, once he flashed his badge.

He looked utterly ridiculous in a Pining for You puffer

jacket with a fluffy bathrobe underneath, and borrowed sweatpants, rubber boots and socks from the manager.

But he didn't want to leave just yet.

He still had questions about the night. Things that didn't quite make sense. But that's not the sole reason why he was here.

Maybe he was being foolish.

Maybe he'd read too much into that kiss.

Maybe. But he was willing to ask, dressed like a clown, and be shot down. Brad had had a point earlier in the evening. He did need to put himself out there.

Maybe Magnolia would say yes.

"I'm not quite dressed yet, Prim. Give me another—" Magnolia opened the door dressed in a full-length fluffy dressing gown, with her hair wrapped in a towel, and fluffy bunny slippers.

Something hot swirled low in his stomach. She looked vulnerable and tired after her eventful night. Still had a little scratch where the mistletoe had landed squarely on her head.

And looked utterly adorable.

"Derek." Her mouth fell open in surprise.

"Were you assaulted or hurt in any way tonight?" he suddenly demanded, clutching a plastic bag at his side.

She cocked her hip and raised an eyebrow. "Other than being attacked by a murder swan?" Magnolia asked drily.

Derek couldn't help by scowl. "I found your leggings and underwear in the snow after the mistletoe hit us. After you took off for Lenny Siddler. I almost lost them in the pond but luckily, they were still in my swan boat after Lenny's arrest. Found your boots too."

He held up the plastic bag and Magnolia took it, her eyes lighting up surprise to see her missing clothing inside.

Her face then softened. "Oh, Derek. No. I'm okay." Her

cheeks flushed pink. "I loaned my clothes to Lenny because he was naked and freezing in the alleyway. I ... shouldn't have been so charitable."

"You had to take off your underwear, too?"

"Spider." Magnolia sucked in her lips and let them out with a pop. "Many spiders. A special kind of winter spider."

"I see." She was a cute liar. He'd give her that.

"Cobwebs came down with the mistletoe off the gutter and ... spiders fell down my top and into my bra. Then, I gave Lenny some clothes. Without the spiders."

"And you're absolutely sure?"

"Yes. Very. I promise I'm okay."

That wasn't a lie. She held his gaze making her promise. Whatever had happened with losing her clothes, he could tell she was adamant she hadn't been hurt or assaulted.

"To tell the truth, I'm buzzing. I haven't felt like this in years. Who knew solving crimes was such a thrill."

Magnolia bounced on the balls of her feet as best she could in fluffy slippers.

Derek chuckled softly. "It is a rush. I made a career out of it."

"Does it always feel like this?"

"Not always. But tonight feels the same way for me too."

He grinned, mirroring hers. His eyes flicked down to her lips. Truth be told it had been more thrilling kissing Magnolia this evening than solving any of the cases he'd worked on the last few years.

As it should be, he thought, dragging his eyes back up to hers.

"But it's not just adrenaline, you know? It's that ... justice won. Something like that."

Her eyes were twinkling. "Yeah, I get that. We had a big night," he murmured. "About the murder swan, as you so put it, Wildlife Control will be here in the morning to remove the swan and her cygnets."

"My manager told me, yes. Has the tiara been returned to the family? Oh." Her face fell. "How are the family? I know Mrs. Astor-Browne had few fans but they lost a loved one tonight. During a wedding of all things."

"She wasn't a guest of the wedding, it turns out. She booked a night here to show off the tiara to the mother of the bride as part of a petty family feud. Bride and groom had no idea." Derek paused. "The Chief of Police has personally seen to Pugsley being matched with a pet sitter in Leavenworth. They're happy to keep him until the family decide where he will live."

"Thanks for letting me know. A big night indeed."

"Your sisters are—"

"Oh god, what did they do?"

"I was going to say protective and fierce about their sister. I only briefly spoke to them to thank them for detaining Lenny. Speaking of ..." Derek paused. "I swear, Lenny ... He looked ..."

He diverted his gaze. How did he explain what he'd seen?

"Looked ...?" Magnolia prompted, frowning.

"Never mind." His mind had played tricks on him, surely. He'd thought Lenny had looked grotesque, like a gangly, hairy monster-like man. "I was avoiding being drowned by a swan. And then there was wrestling with mistletoe in my face."

Magnolia reached up and brushed his fringe from his forehead. "It left a mark on you, too."

Derek's breathing hitched. He felt like a giddy teenager rather than a forty-year-old divorcee.

"I need to go. Wedding guests and a bridal couple to catch up with."

"Oh, of course."

He hesitated on the spot, staring at his shoes. *Just do it, man.*

"It was an unexpectedly good kiss in the midst of all the drama tonight," she blurted.

Derek glanced back up just as her hair towel began to unravel and she quickly swept it up.

Now or never.

"Would you like to get a coffee with me sometime?" Derek asked in a rush.

"Like, a date?"

"Not if you don't want it to be. I'd just love to talk with you over a coffee. But if you'd like a date, that's great too."

"I'd like that."

Derek's mouth pulled into a smile, transforming his face from a broody grump to one of delight.

"How's tomorrow?"

"Fine."

"10.30 a.m.? At the Gingerbread House in Leavenworth?"

"It's a date, Detective Deveney."

A DATE.

Magnolia grinned, brushing her hair, now dressed. She was going on a date. Tomorrow.

With the man who had made her toes curl with a kiss.

And she had used magic – made magic? Magic had used her?

Her familiar was back, sort of.

Nothing on her part after her shower and changing into a spare uniform had replicated the transformation into her familiar's form.

Not even with more mistletoe, she thought, scowling at

several red dots on her fingertips where she'd pricked the thorns, hoping to conjure Gordon back.

Where were her sisters? Should she tell them about Derek and the date?

If they were going to head home, they needed to make tracks asap—

Her phone rang, shrill in the silence of the cabin.

Usually Prim texted, as she hated making calls.

"Hey Prim, I'm good to go when you are—"

"Magnolia." The use of her full name and the tone of her sister's voice made Magnolia heart leap.

"What's wrong?" If Lenny had—

"It's Aggie."

The anguish in Prim's voice made Magnolia sit up straight. "Aggie? What's happened?"

"She's ... someone has ... Geri is coming to your cabin to get you. I've taken one of the farm trucks to Wanatchee General to be with her. Noah has promised to speak to a doctor or someone to find out more—"

Thank the goddess that Prim was dating Noah, a normie, who worked at the hospital as a children's nurse.

But why would her Aunt Agapanthus, a powerful witch, need an ambulance?

"What the hell has happened?"

"She was attacked. At the close of the dinner service at Witches' Brew. She's unconscious. The kitchen has been declared a crime scene and she's been taken to hospital."

The ominous feeling of storm clouds on the horizon washed over her.

With Prim's words, it felt like the storm was breaking right now at her door.

Magnolia woke with a snort as Aggie's sister, Aunt Aspidistra, swept into the hospital ward.

"Cheese graters," Aggie muttered, pulling her bedsheet up higher.

Machines beeped, monitoring Aggie's vital signs.

She had woken up in the ambulance on the way to Wanatchee General. But could only now say two words.

Cheese graters.

Doctors had been convinced she had a concussion that had affected the language part of the brain.

But she and her sisters were convinced it was something magically induced, even if Aggie did have a large cut and bump on the back of her head.

Magnolia had been awake all night by Aggie's bedside and early morning. She couldn't have dozed off for more than an hour or so.

"Cheese. Graters," Aggie muttered again, somehow managing to make the only two words in her repertoire very expressive.

"Agapanthus," Aunt Aspidistra said simply, standing straight and tall, and looking over her sister with a critical eye.

Her long grey hair flowing faultlessly straight down her back. Magnolia and her sisters had joked that Aunt Aspy (only said behind her back) had made a pact with the Devil to get hair that flawless.

"Mags, Aunt Aspy is—oh." Geri came to an abrupt halt in the doorway with Prim careering into her from behind. "Oof! I mean Aunt Aspidistra has arrived from England. As you can see."

Aspidistra gave Geri a withering look while Magnolia wiped at the corners of her mouth in case of drool while sleeping.

She shook her head, hoping to clear the fog of her nap.

Aspidistra then turned her steel gaze back on Aggie, who stared back silently, somehow communicating something beyond the power of words.

"Your powers came back today," Aspidistra said sharply.

Magnolia jumped, not expecting the focus to be on her. She sat up in the chair, smoothing her rumpled clothes.

"Aunt Aspidistra, hello." Magnolia cleared her throat. Ugh, her breath. "Briefly, and then they went away again."

"Explain."

Magnolia glanced at Aggie. The focus should be on her aunt, not her, but Aggie nodded quickly, encouraging her to answer Aspidistra.

"I thought of fire and held a diamond tiara in the pond and made it boil." Aspidistra blinked. "And I turned into my familiar's form after I stabbed myself with mistletoe."

Aspidistra seemed unruffled but her eyes were swirling. "What happened before this? Leave out nothing."

"Well, in truth, I'd been assaulted by a mistletoe missile—"

"Mistletoe missile?" Aspidistra asked, stepping forward.

"Um, yes, Aunt. I made garlands of three kinds of mistletoe for a wedding at a Christmas tree farm," Geri said, fidgeting with her corsage.

"European mistletoe?"

Prim nodded. "Yes, and North American and a third variety as well. Grown at the orchard."

"Ahh, how fortuitous for you, Magnolia, that your sister's botanical knowledge should have been employed for wedding decorations."

There was a moment where the three sisters glanced at each other, unsure if Aunt Aspidistra had made a compliment or an insult.

Aspidistra turned, sweeping her long black skirt around, and paced the small room that Aggie had been put in.

"Armies have gathered under mistletoe to call a truce. And it is a traditional Yule decoration, reminding us of the color of summer and plenty on the longest night. And, of course, romance." Aspidistra paused as if that word pained her to say. "As well as healing."

She narrowed her eyes at Magnolia. "Did the mistletoe scratch you?"

Magnolia's hand flew up to the mark on her forehead. "I think so. But I was preoccupied with murder swans and were-raccoons at the time."

"Were-*what?*" Aspidistra spluttered.

"That was my thought too. Lenny Siddler, who took me to the prom. He's a were-raccoon. Said that there were many things us witches didn't know in Leavenworth."

"Were you aware of this Lenny being a were-creature in your senior year?"

"Nope. Pretty sure he wasn't in high school. And I didn't get a chance to ask how he'd become a were-coon."

Aspidistra huffed and her steely gaze flicked back to Magnolia's forehead.

"And you changed into your familiar's form? Like a glamour spell?"

"No, more like we were sharing the same cat body. I could hear my familiar and communicate with him. It felt like I was shoved inside a too small costume."

Aspidistra inhaled a deep breath. "So your familiar is back."

"Not quite? I tried to replicate bringing Gordon back with different mistletoe later but nothing worked."

"The most primal of all magic. Blood magic."

Aspidistra and Aggie shared a look again, and Aggie nodded.

"A plant used to bring armies to peace, for love to bloom ..." Aspidistra rolled her eyes. "And for its use in heart and blood medicine for centuries, and last but not least, a symbol of hope and joy during Yule, the dark times, made you bleed."

"Derek was cut as well."

Aspidistra blinked, sneering. "Who or what is Derek?"

Magnolia blushed, squirming under her aunt's scrutiny. She hadn't anticipated a pop quiz by her aunt when no one knew why Aggie couldn't speak beyond 'cheese graters'.

"The detective. He helped me catch Lenny." Magnolia swallowed hard, not wishing to share the kiss. Not yet. "He was also under the mistletoe."

"Huh. I see." Aspidistra sighed and then became thoughtful. "It was a full moon as well last night."

"Hence the were-coon incident with Lenny."

"But also enhancing all magic performed on the darkest night."

Aspidistra and Aggie once again met each other's gaze. Aggie's usual jovial face was stoic and hard. Aspidistra was uncharacteristically sad.

An orderly appeared with a trolley of food trays. "Lunch service. Sorry I'm late."

Aggie clapped her hands together, eager for the selection of hospital food.

"Wait, lunch?" Magnolia scrambled to find her phone. "What time is it?"

"Almost one." Geri's face fell. "Oh Mags, you missed it."

"Missed what?" Aspidistra asked, in a clipped tone.

"I was going to meet Derek for coffee at 10.30am."

"The same Derek as the mistletoe incident?"

"Yes." One o'clock! How had she napped for so long. It was no use. Leavenworth was thirty minutes away from Wanatchee General Hospital. "He's long gone now."

"A shame. We could have asked him questions about the mistletoe incident to learn more of what happened that you had a spontaneous return of your powers."

Magnolia looked away. She'd been looking forward to coffee and chatting.

Funny how one kiss had made her want to reconsider dating again.

Cher had sung about how *'it's in his kiss, that's where it is'*.

One kiss and being bopped on the head by weaponized wedding decorations had resulted being briefly reunited with her familiar, using magic again, and now what? Nothing. No clue how it happened.

Her hand slipped into her pocket and she felt the business card of Dawson and McIntyre Private Investigators.

"But this isn't about me. We need to focus on Aggie. Sure we can test for hexes, or other spells, maybe a twist on a mute spell?"

"It's been done." Aspidistra waved her hand dismissively. "Agapanthus is not hexed, nor under any spell of another."

Magnolia stood from the chair, her foot brushing against

something hard. The Yule log of cherrywood was beside her bag under the chair. They hadn't made it back to Witches Brew in time to burn it on Solstice.

No doubt Witches Brew was a crime scene right now.

"How do we know Aggie isn't hexed? We haven't even had a chance to test this—"

She paused, glancing at her sisters who had guilt written all over their faces.

"You tested for hexes without me?"

"I'm sorry, Magnolia." Prim took after Aspidistra with her cold stare but now she looked sad. "You'd finally got to sleep just after six and Geri and I did some spells before the doctor's round to see if we could detect any hex or wards."

Magnolia's heart sank.

"And you found nothing?"

"Cheese graters," Aggie piped up, throwing her hands in the air and making the two words sound like 'zip, zilch'.

"But writing—"

"No matter what we tried, Aggie can only write cheese graters as well, no matter what we ask of her, no matter if it's pen and paper, or a digital device or laptop." Geri threw up her hands. "We're waiting to see what the doctors say later today. They are taking Aggie in for brain scans and other tests."

Aspidistra sniffed. "Useless activity Aggie has to endure in order to be discharged."

Prim frowned. "Noah will keep an eye on her results. And we won't leave her side. Especially when the police come today to take her statement."

"Cheese graters," Aggie muttered.

It was going to be a short statement. Magnolia leaned on the hospital bed, and felt Aggie's forehead.

Everything about her aunt felt and looked fine. Except 'cheese graters'.

The bed felt gritty under her other hand, and she rubbed her fingers together and held them up to her sisters. "Salt?"

Both Geri and Prim looked sheepish, each of them glancing at Aspidistra. "A salt circle for protection."

"This is for me as well as Aggie, isn't it?"

Her sisters and Aspidistra all nodded. Aggie patted her hand.

"If this Lenny character knew you were a witch, and someone has attacked Aggie at Witches Brew by our family hearth, I will set up wards and protection spells, as well as draw up as many salt circles as we need." Aspidistra adjusted her black corset and stared down her long nose at each of them, settling on Magnolia. "No one crossed the Moone family without consequences. We will find those who did this, and we will find this were-raccoon and question him."

Despite the shock of the last twenty-four hours, her aunt's words lifted Magnolia's spirits. She felt armored, ready for battle.

"I'll care for Aunt Aggie. I already live in her apartment. And I'll take on the brewing at Witches Brew under her instruction. We'll get to the bottom of this, I promise, aunt."

Murder swans and were-coons felt like the tip of the iceberg for Magnolia's future but with her family by her side, she felt she had allies to face the oncoming storm.

EPILOGUE
8 FEBRUARY

Magnolia let out an involuntary sigh as Brad strolled into Witches Brew.

He blew a low whistle as he circled her with an exaggerated swagger. "Well, hi there, Maggie. Looking fine as usual."

She cocked an eyebrow, sighing again. "Here for your usual—"

He clicked his fingers and pointed finger guns her way, cutting her off. "Brisket special, Maggie. Please and thank you."

Brad finished his order with a wink.

Ugh. "Sure thing."

She hesitated before delivering his order to the kitchen. "So, um. Any update about Lenny Siddler and his theft before Christmas?"

"Oh yeah, I do." Brad clicked his fingers again. "Just this morning it came through to the precinct that his case will be heard in court next week."

Lenny hadn't been seen or heard of since his arrest.

Magnolia made a mental note to look up the court hearings and perhaps hang around to bump into Lenny for a little chat about his were-raccoon status.

Brad clicked his fingers a third time, startling Magnolia out of her thoughts of interrogation techniques.

"Got a new detective starting so that means I'll have more time off to socialize and so forth. Like … Valentine's Day, for example." He waggled his eyebrows but Maggie was unmoved. Sure, Valentine's Day was coming up in six days but she had no intention of spending it with Brad.

The deputy cleared his throat and continued. "So, uh, the new guy's name is …"

Metal pans crashed in the kitchen and followed by cursing in cheese graters, muting Brad's words.

But Magnolia's heart skipped a beat. *Did he just say Derek?* Memories of mistletoe and swans bubbled to the surface of her mind.

And of toe-curling kisses. "Did you just—"

"Oh my goddess!" Geri screamed as she stormed into Witches Brew, her copper hair streaming behind her, with Aggie hot on her heels. Several customers glanced their way but neither of them paid any attention. "This has got to be a joke!"

"What—" Magnolia started but was cut off as Geri held up a letter, like it was a bag of dog poop.

"This cannot be true!"

Aggie nodded, pointing at the letter with a deep scowl.

Magnolia slowly took it from Geri's vice-like grip between her index finger and thumb and Prim joined them from the bar.

"Something's got Geri's knickers in a knot," chuckled the deputy.

Both Magnolia and Prim shot him glares that could have

caused a mini-ice age. He stammered an excuse to go back to his lunch.

"Eviction?" Prim muttered over Magnolia's shoulder. "What in the gates of hell?"

Magnolia's heartrate skipped faster as she skimmed over the letter, noting a logo for a legal firm.

Notice to evict. Rent in arrears. Several decades owed to our client, Consolidated Jaeger Industries.

"But we own Witches Brew," Magnolia said, somewhat breathless. "Don't we?"

"We do." Prim's tone brooked no argument, but she frowned. "I don't recall our parents ever saying we were tenants. A Moone witch has brewed at this spot for over one hundred years."

"The solicitors are real on that letter," Geri spit, stabbing the offensive pages in Magnolia's hands with her index finger. "I was going to do my internship with them for my law degree."

"You're studying law?" Prim asked, incredulous, as if Geri studying a degree was more outrageous than being evicted in thirty days.

Geri paled and shrugged.

But something caught Magnolia's eye at the bottom of the letter, diverting all thoughts of Geri's covert legal studies to impending doom.

"It says if we don't pay for decades of owed rent, we have thirty days to leave the property." Magnolia looked up, dazed, noting the date on the letter. "Witches Brew could be gone in a less than a month."

Happy Valentine's Day, indeed.

THE END

. . .

Research notes:

Murders swans are a Thing. I was sitting in a café with Ally Blake and Kali Anthony, each of us writing our WIPs. I tumbled down a rabbithole of murderous swans who are on record for beating up people with their wings and preventing them from surfacing to drown them.

Upon discovering murder swans were a Thing, and subjecting Ally and Kali to many anecdotes of swans knocking off people, I had to capture this in a story.

This story was published as "Seven Swans are Swimming" in the "My True Love Gave to Me" anthology in 2023 but it was always called "Murder Swans" in my heart.

The next Magnolia Moone mystery, A Cadaver for my Valentine, is coming February 2025!

Sign up for my newsletter to be informed of new releases and her latest news.

ABOUT THE AUTHOR

Sabrina Duval is a Buffy tragic who likes her vampires and werewolves to crack jokes and be a little morally grey. She lives between Brisbane and thirty-five acres of serenity in the Granite Belt region of Queensland with her family and a fat cattle dog-Kelpie cross. Her local rural fire brigade inspired her to start writing small town romcoms under the name Louisa Duval.

As Louisa, her novels have finaled in the Australian Association of Romance Readers for best banter and dialogue, and Romance Writers of NZ's Koru for Long Romance. She was a part of Queensland Writers Centre's *Adaptable* program to pitch her stories to film and TV producers and came second in Romance Writers of Australia's 2022 Spicy Bites '*Machines*' competition with her short story '*Vintage Love Machines*'. She was also published in Romance Writers of Australia's 2021 Sweet Treats '*Chocolate*' Anthology with her short story '*Chocolate and Orange*'. The anthology won the Australian Romance Readers Association's Members Choice Award for Favorite Romance Anthology in 2021.

Louisa and Sabrina send a monthly newsletter with bonus editions with bookish news and latest releases. Sign up to the newsletter using the QR code below and follow Sabrina on Instagram (@sabrinaduvalwriter)

www.ingramcontent.com/pod-product-compliance
Lightning Source LLC
Chambersburg PA
CBHW021935170626
46807CB00007B/3127